CREEP

"  "

—Sydney V., 9, Murfreesboro

"These books are good stories that you will want to read. Not too creepy, but scary enough!"

—Owen H., 10, Mansfield

"Creepers is an amazing series that keeps me turning pages well past my bedtime (sorry mom)!"

—@pageturningpatrick, 11, Collingwood

"I wanted to keep reading, I didn't know what was going to happen next! It was exciting and creepy all at the same time!"

—Avery H., 12, Hamilton

"Creepers is creepy, fun, and a bit mesmerizing!"

—Clara H., 10, Burlington

"The suspense kept me going! I can't wait to read the next book!!"

—Francesca N., 12, Jackson Heights

"The characters are very intriguing, and the ending of the book was unpredictable."

—Abby, 11, Murfreesboro

"Those of the younger audience will get a cold shiver down their back while reading this book, as the same happened to me once or twice."

—Cameron, 13, Smyrna

Cold Kisser

by Edgar J. Hyde

Illustrations by Chloe Tyler

PAB-0608-0298 • ISBN: 978-1-4867-1874-0

Copyright ©2020 Flowerpot Press, a Division of Flowerpot Children's Press, Inc., Oakville, ON, Canada.

Printed and bound in the U.S.A.

Table of Contents

CHAPTER ONE

A Ventriloquist

Tommy McDonald was what his classmates called ordinary. He didn't hang out with the tough guys, and he didn't have girls lining up to ask him out on dates.

"I'm only fourteen! There's plenty of time for all that," he'd reply when being teased by boys like George Borden. George was only fourteen too, but he had kissed five girls! At least! Anyway, that's what he said.

"You got any witnesses to these kisses, George?" Tommy would say.

"Witnesses—I prefer to kiss girls in private, not for a bunch of people to stand and cheer!"

"Well, how do I know you're not making it all up?"

"Just ask Lisa, or Lyndsey, or Jane...should I go on...?"

"Okay, okay," Tommy would reply, knowing full well that he'd never ask Lisa, Lyndsey, or any other girl if she'd been kissed by George.

Tommy was feeling left out and George's confidence with girls made him feel childish by comparison.

Tommy was dreading this year's prom. This would be the big event for all those in Tommy's grade to celebrate—if that's the right word—completing the first year at the intimidating Moorborne High School.

Being a quiet type, Tommy had left all the mischief to the other boys in his class. He'd watched, with little interest, as they fought with each other and tried to impress—or even kiss—the girls. Some of his classmates seemed to think the point of school was to do your best not to be taught anything at all, and to disrupt the class so that no one else could learn either.

Tommy preferred to work hard, even do his homework and pass tests! The other boys often wondered what was wrong with him. Luckily for Tommy, he was nearly six feet tall, despite only being fourteen.

On the few occasions any of the tough guys, like Ronnie Ryan, picked a fight with him, Tommy would fight back. Even though he lost a few fights, the Ronnie Ryans of the school eventually decided it was more trouble than it was worth to pick on Tommy.

Tommy wasn't the smartest in his class. He had to work hard for his grades. But he did work hard. He wanted to be a reporter for a big newspaper when he left school and knew he needed qualifications. Fighting, teasing girls, detentions—these were for the clowns like Ronnie Ryan. Nothing was going to distract Tommy from his aim in life. Nothing. Tommy lived only a street away from the school. George Borden used to be his next-door neighbor until George's dad got a new job and his family moved. George was now one of the boys who took the school bus home. This gave him plenty of after-school gossip to share with Tommy when they sat beside each other in English class.

"George," said Tommy after English one day, "you should be a ventriloquist when you finish school."

"Why?"

"Because, all through the English class you talked nonstop. I'm sure Mrs. Gray heard your voice, but she never saw your lips move."

"Of course not," said George proudly. "I practice in front of the mirror every night—when you're doing your homework, I guess!"

"What for?"

"Because I never get to see you besides in English. You never come out after school. You spend all your time in the library. You should live for now not for the future, then I wouldn't have to do all the talking. Then you might do things worth talking about."

"What, like kissing girls, running around after school with a football...great, huh? Don't you ever worry about the future, or what you might do after school?" inquired Tommy.

"Yeah, after school I'm taking Maggie Allen down to the mall," replied George.

"No, I mean after, after school—when you're eighteen, when you're finally grown up—what are you going to be?" persisted Tommy.

"A ventriloquist—and because you've got nothing useful to say, you'd make a great dummy! See you tomorrow, Tommy," said George as he ran off to catch the school bus home. George was smiling and Tommy found it hard not to smile back.

"See you tomorrow, you weirdo," shouted Tommy.

CHAPTER TWO

New Girl

"Now," said Miss Sharpe, as the class settled into their chairs.

Tommy sat on his own with a vacant seat beside him. The desks were arranged as follows: three long columns of desks were stretched from the front of the classroom to the back. Each column had five double desks, one behind the other. So most pupils sat beside another boy or girl.

Tommy sat at the middle desk in the row closest to the large windows. The double desk behind him was completely empty, and Ronnie Ryan sat at the desk behind the empty one. Ronnie was considered such a bad influence that he sat alone in most classes, always in the back. Most teachers appeared to have given up on him and decided to seat him as far away from the rest of the class as possible.

Unknown to the teachers, this merely gave Ronnie a great opportunity to stock up on paper bullets. Ronnie would take the ink part out of his pen and put the point end into his mouth. Then he'd put a piece of crumpled up paper, which he called his bullet, into the other end of the pen. Throughout most lessons, kids who Ronnie didn't like, and that was most of them, would feel a slight sting on the back of their heads. They all knew that the cause of this annoyance was Ronnie and his paper bullets. But the code of silence, which exists in all classrooms and forbids too much cooperation with teachers, was always at work. So the teachers were unaware of this particular vice of Ronnie's.

"Now," said Miss Sharpe, again, trying to live up to her name. "I want silence right now!" Gradually the rumblings and mutterings died down and Miss

Sharpe could be heard.

The students could see a beautiful girl standing beside Miss Sharpe at the front of the room, looking a little nervous, obviously waiting to be introduced.

"Before I call roll, I'd like to introduce a new student. This is Sally Anne Dickens."

A few wolf whistles went up from the boys in the room. The girl named Sally Anne Dickens blushed. Her red face contrasted dramatically with her beautiful long straight blonde hair, which was down to her waist. She was very tall, taller than any other girl in the class. She was immaculately dressed and looked every inch the young lady. But Tommy could sense that the girl was very embarrassed and probably wanted to be sitting anonymously at a desk, not standing up in front of the class as the new kid, an awful label for anyone, thought Tommy, especially someone who is shy!

Tommy immediately felt attracted to Sally Anne. What boy wouldn't be?

Miss Sharpe had finished the introductions and now asked Sally Anne to sit down at one of the vacant desks.

Tommy's heart beat faster as she walked toward, he thought, the vacant desk behind him.

Oh no, thought Tommy. Sit somewhere else, please! Although she was the first girl who had ever caught his attention, she made him so nervous that he really wished she would sit somewhere else.

Tommy tried not to notice her as she got closer to his desk, then closer. Tommy's head was face down as he pretended to be engrossed in his notebook. But he was aware of her as she reached his desk. He waited for her to keep walking to the desk behind him. But instead she stopped. Then Tommy realized that she was looking at the vacant seat beside him!

Surely she would choose to sit at a double desk all to herself rather than share one with Tommy, who was, after all, a stranger! But she was still standing beside him. He felt the full stare of everyone in the

class as they turned around to see where Sally Anne was going to sit. Then she spoke.

"Excuse me," she said.

Tommy's red face looked up and said, "Y-Y-Yes?"

"Is anyone sitting here?" she said softly.

"Er..."

"No, Sally Anne," interrupted Miss Sharpe. "No one is sitting there. I'm sure Tommy will move his backpack off that chair for you, won't you Tommy?"

"Of course," said Tommy, trying to recover from the embarrassment. "Of course, please, sit down," he said removing his backpack. But he hadn't closed it all the way that morning and all his books, pens, and notebooks fell out all over the floor. He bent under the desk to pick them up.

Then he heard George shout from the front of the classroom, "He's looking up her skirt!"

The class erupted in laughter. Tommy was now dripping with sweat, bright red, and utterly embarrassed. On hearing George's joke, he tried to stand up quickly, forgetting that he was under his desk. The loud thud of Tommy's head hitting the desk produced another series of laughs from his classmates.

"That's enough," said Miss Sharpe, trying not to laugh. "Really, Tommy, can't you pick them up later?"

Tommy wanted the ground to open up and swallow him right there. As the laughter was finally dying down, Sally Anne sat down beside him.

Why me? wondered Tommy. Miss Sharpe was walking back over to her desk to call roll. Sally Anne didn't seem to be embarrassed at all. Maybe she was glad that Tommy had unwittingly stolen the show and distracted attention away from her. But Tommy was sure when she caught his eye as she sat down, she smiled at him.

That was the first class of the semester that Tommy could not completely remember. It was the first time he had not heard one word. In fact, when the bell rang signaling the end of class, Tommy was so out of it that he wondered if he'd been there at all.

CHAPTER THREE

Tell Me

"What's she like, Tommy?" muttered George in English class later that day in his best ventriloquist style. No answer.

"Come on, she's gorgeous. What's she like?" he persisted. Still silence.

"Oh, here we go again. Tommy the dumbstruck dummy with nothing to say. The most beautiful girl in the school decides to sit next to him and he still has nothing to say. Should I do both parts, Tommy? 'Well, George,'" said George, imitating Tommy's deep voice, "'it's like this, I'm full of animal magnetism—girls can't resist me...'"

"Shut up, George," snapped Tommy angrily.

"Tommy, I'm joking. But if you're not interested in kissing Sally Anne, that's just as well because you'd have to join a line a mile long—with me at the front!" said George, laughing without moving his lips. Tommy said nothing.

Tommy didn't go to the library that morning. He'd decided to go looking for Sally Anne. Not to talk—no, nothing as brave as that—just to look at her. She was pretty. He couldn't get her out of his mind.

When George saw Tommy later, he broke off from his game of football to talk to him.

"You okay, Tommy?" he asked.

"Yeah, why wouldn't I be?" Tommy said emphatically.

"All right, all right. You look lost, that's all."

They saw Sally Anne talking to some of the girls from class over by the stairs.

"Let's go and introduce ourselves," said George,

walking over to where Sally Anne was standing.

"Wha-what will we say?" asked Tommy nervously.

"You say what you're good at saying, Tommy—nothing. When it comes to girls, you're the dummy, remember?" replied George.

Was George going to set Tommy up on a date with Sally Anne? Did he have a master plan worked out to bring these two soul mates together? wondered Tommy. Soul mates, thought Tommy. He wondered if there was really such a thing. The more he thought of Sally Anne, the more he thought, okay, so now I'm interested in girls. Now what?

As they approached the group of girls that included Sally Anne, Tommy felt his nerves ease. Now that he'd admitted to himself that he liked her, all he had to do was talk to her—gulp! He panicked.

"You do the talking, genius," he pleaded to George.

"Okay—I'm going to," George replied.

George had no idea that Tommy liked Sally Anne. George was going to do the talking because he liked Sally Anne, too.

"Hey, Sally Anne, I'll make room beside me in class if you like," he said.

"No, no," she blushed, shocked at George's upfront opening line.

"It's okay, really."

Tommy was livid, his best friend, his only real friend, was talking to his girl.

"Really," George persisted. "I'll tie up Jimmy Leach, who sits beside me, and leave him in the bathroom. You and me have lots to talk about, sweetheart."

Sally Anne was mildly amused. George was obviously charming and harmless. But she really wanted Tommy to be the one making the moves, after all, that's why she'd sat down beside him in class. She'd seen him through the crowd as the class arrived that morning. He was tall like her. She felt embarrassed looking down at boys like George. It made her feel old. She was only fourteen after all. But Tommy had no idea what she was thinking.

And because Tommy was silent, Sally Anne thought he wasn't interested. He must be here just to back up George, she thought.

"Can I buy you a romantic lunch sometime?" said George.

"Can you buy me romantic lunch?" she repeated, amazed. She continued, "Is there a fancy restaurant nearby?"

"No," George was a bit annoyed. I'll tell the jokes, he thought. "What about we just share my sandwich at lunch?"

"Only if you have smoked salmon and caviar," she joked.

"Great," said George, "I'll bring the champagne— or as it's known in these parts—Diet Coke!"

"Cafeteria at 12:30?" she asked, almost disinterestedly.

"Done."

"See you then, big spender," she laughed.

"That's how it's done." George grinned as he saw Tommy looking at him. "What's wrong, don't you want to learn how to get girls? I'm not even charging you for the lesson!"

George had been hit hard a few times before. Ronnie Ryan's fist had hit George's jaw on numerous occasions. Sometimes George could joke his way out of it and sometimes he couldn't. Today, as he fell after Tommy's punch landed square on his chest, he knew it was one of those times he couldn't.

"Get up," said Tommy menacingly.

Realizing that Tommy wanted to hit him again, George, remembering, among other things, his own height was barely five feet, replied, "You're joking, right?"

"Get up," said Tommy menacingly. "Maybe you need a boxing lesson. Maybe you're not so smart after all." Tommy's face was blue with rage. He was nearly crying as he shouted at George, who was still on the ground.

❄   ❄   ❄

Of course, news of Tommy's outburst traveled around the school.

George didn't speak to Tommy the next day in English. In fact, Sally Anne had sat behind Tommy in class that morning after giving him a dirty look. I bet they've been talking about me, thought Tommy. He was ashamed of hitting George, but most of all, he was ashamed of not having the courage to talk to Sally Anne.

It was Tommy, then, who broke the silence near the end of English class.

"Well, did she meet your kissing standards?" asked Tommy sarcastically.

"What...?" replied George vaguely.

Tommy saw George rubbing his chest and felt sorry that he'd hit him. "George, I don't know what came over me yesterday."

"What are you talking about, Tommy?"

"When I hit you—"

"Oh that," said George, as if he'd been thinking of something else. "Don't worry about it, Tommy. I don't mean to be that way, but I know I am sometimes."

"I thought you weren't speaking to me because of our fight yesterday," said Tommy.

There was a long pause until George whispered, "It's not that. I kissed Sally Anne."

"Oh!" said Tommy loud enough for Mrs. Gray to hear.

"No talking, Tommy," she said. "It's bad enough that you didn't do your homework last night and were fighting yesterday, but do you have to distract George too? Really, what's wrong with you lately? Back to work!"

"I won't be kissing her again," said George quietly after Mrs. Gray turned her head.

"Why not?" asked Tommy.

"Have you heard of that spider in South America. You know, the female that paralyzes the male with a bite, then kills him?" For once George's joking tone appeared to have deserted him.

"Eh, I'm not sure."

"Well, I was walking her back to class after lunch. We'd just shared my roast beef…"

"Oh, very classy. Way to impress a champagne lady!" laughed Tommy.

"…sandwich when I decided the moment was right to kiss her."

"What happened? With all your experience? Did you pick the wrong moment? Did your moves fail you? Did your scientific method of deciding the right moment let you down?"

"No, it was the right moment. But…" George broke off.

"But what?" asked Tommy now very interested.

"Well, it's kind of spooky."

"Don't tell me you were scared, champion kisser."

George paused then said, "I-I was."

The bell rang for the end of class. As they filed out, Tommy said to George, "Let's go hang out somewhere. I gotta hear this."

"You mean skip the next class?"

"Yeah, I want the story. I'm a little spooked myself about this girl," said Tommy.

Both George and Tommy knew that they'd be missed in art class and that they'd have some explaining to do, but they went and found a spot under the stairs anyway.

"So, George, tell me about this kiss."

Again George hesitated. "Well, I kinda—," he searched for the right word, "froze, I guess."

"Froze, I guess," repeated Tommy. "Sounds like the moves of a pro."

"It's not funny, Tommy. I reached out and held her. She seemed to think it was a good idea. And I kissed her. But her lips felt so cold."

"How? It's almost summer."

"Exactly, but that wasn't all. Her lips weren't cold, they were freezing. My mind went blank. I couldn't move. I couldn't think. Not only had my own lips become cold, but the air felt cold and I remember thinking this is what it must feel like to kiss a ghost."

"A ghost," gasped Tommy.

"Yeah, a ghost. I mean, I don't believe in all that stuff, but it was freaky."

"Are you sure you weren't imagining all this?" asked Tommy sarcastically.

"I thought so at first, because in my mind I started to see all sorts of things from another time."

"What do you mean?" inquired Tommy.

"No, it's too weird, you won't believe me."

Tommy leaned back against the wall, distracted by what George was saying. He was wondering whether or not to let George in on his little secret. A secret that he barely understood himself, but since George had been talking it all began to make sense.

"I do believe you, George" said Tommy, breaking

the awkward silence.

"You do? Why? If you'd told me this bizarre story, I don't think I would have believed you."

Here goes nothing, thought Tommy, as he prepared to tell George his secret.

"Do you promise not to tell anyone about what I'm about to tell you?" asked Tommy.

"Okay."

"Well, the day before Sally Anne showed up in our class, I had a dream about a beautiful girl and when I first saw Sally Anne, she reminded me so much of this beautiful girl. I thought she was the same girl but that couldn't be...could it?"

"Go on," encouraged George.

"In the dream she said, 'I'm coming for you. We have unfinished business. You have to let me help you.' But whenever I asked her what it was she had to help me with she just looked frightened and said, 'Don't you remember?'

"In the dream she was familiar to me but I

couldn't remember where I'd seen her before. In fact, she was offended that I couldn't remember. I woke up saying, 'Tell me.'

"I tried to just forget about it. When I saw her the next day, supposedly for the first time, I decided that it was just a coincidence that she looked like the girl in my dream."

"A dream?" George interrupted. "That's what it was like when I kissed her. Like I was in a dream."

At that moment, they both stopped talking. They heard footsteps on the stairs. It was Sally Anne.

As she approached, she smiled at them.

Worried and confused, the boys smiled back unconvincingly.

"Mr. Bush is asking where you are," she said, "both of you."

CHAPTER FOUR

The Painting

Mr. Bush was called "Mr. Brush" by the students because it sounded more fitting for an art teacher. He also lost his temper a lot, which was scary. The kids sometimes called him "Old Burning," as in burning bush. He was only forty-two but to his students anything over sixteen was old, so forty-two years old was definitely old. Meaning Old Burning Bush was old *and* scary.

When George and Tommy walked into the classroom with only ten minutes remaining, Old Burning let them have it.

"I'm responsible for you while you're supposed to be in my class. If anything happened to you I'd get in big trouble," he shouted.

"It's nice of you to show such concern for us, Old Burn...I mean, Mr. Bush," said George.

Mr. Bush told them to take their seats and just do nothing for the remaining minutes of class.

"George," whispered Tommy.

"What?"

"Look at Sally Anne's painting."

Some students in the art class had obviously been painting a bunch of flowers.

"I hope you've enjoyed your lesson in still life," Mr. Bush remarked.

"It doesn't look still alive to me," shouted Ronnie Ryan, to much laughter.

"Keep your mouth shut, Ryan, unless you want to stay after class," growled Old Burning.

"I'd stay here all right, Mr. Bush. After all, you've explained how you're responsible for my wellbeing while I'm in your class," said Ronnie sarcastically.

"Exactly—while you're in my class. I didn't say

anything about what could happen to you outside my class, did I?" replied Mr. Bush threateningly.

Ronnie shut up.

Once this minor commotion died down, George did what Tommy had previously asked and looked at Sally Anne's painting. It looked great. Why had Tommy asked him to look at it though, thought George. Neither of them cared about art.

"So?" asked George outside the art class as students fought to get out in the fresh air.

"So?" replied Tommy. "Does nothing strike you as odd about the painting?"

George thought about it before replying. "Well, she painted a village instead of those silly begonias, and I would have used a lighter shade of gray for the sky," he said sarcastically. "What do I know about paintings? What was odd about it?"

"It was finished, wasn't it?"

"Yes, so what?"

"Sally Anne's painting was the only one that was

finished in class."

"Get to the point, Tommy."

"Well, how could she have had time to finish it? After all, didn't she come to find us to tell us that Mr. Bush was waiting for us?"

"Yeah, but she got back before us, remember? She ran on ahead of us back to the class," replied George.

"But we were on the other side of the school—and she had to find us."

"What are you getting at, Tommy?"

"And she stood talking to us—or should I say, you—for about five minutes."

"And still managed to get back to class and finish that painting?" asked George.

"Exactly—there wasn't enough time."

"Unless she happens to be a gifted artist," said George sarcastically.

"She'd need to be better and quicker than anyone else. I mean, Lucy Stevenson is the best by far—right?" asked Tommy.

"Yeah..."

"Well, even she didn't finish on time."

"So? Sally Anne's good at art—big deal," said George, losing interest in the conversation.

"See you tomorrow," he said as he ran to catch the school bus home.

Tommy walked home slowly, with a puzzled expression on his face. He heard footsteps behind him and when he looked back he was surprised to see Sally Anne catching up to him.

"Hi, Tommy," she said.

CHAPTER FIVE

The Visit

"I hope Mr. Bush didn't scare you too much," she said mockingly.

"I can see why you and George get along so well—you both think you have a sense of humor," said Tommy.

"What else do you think we have in common?" she asked, sensing Tommy was a little annoyed.

"Neither of you are funny," said Tommy as he continued walking.

"There's no need to be rude, Tommy."

"I didn't think you were talking to me anyway. I thought you were siding with your kissing partner after I hit him."

"I know," she said thoughtfully.

"Well, this is where I live," said Tommy at his gate.

"Aren't you going to invite me in for a soda?" she said laughing.

Tommy was surprised. "Why?" he said curiously.

"Because we have a lot to talk about."

Tommy couldn't remember inviting her in exactly but there he was, pouring her soda over ice and nervously offering her cookies.

But he felt very comfortable with her. He couldn't explain it.

Then she came right out with it.

"Tommy, keep this to yourself, but I'm a witch."

Tommy stared at her from his seat as she calmly sipped her drink.

"Great cookies, Tommy. Homemade?"

Tommy just stared.

"Don't say you hadn't guessed," she said.

Tommy then started to giggle. "Let me guess,

you're here to tell me my future?" He caught himself quickly but still had trouble stopping. Don't laugh in her face, he thought. She might actually believe that she is a witch. After all, George thinks he's a comedian, Mr. Bush thinks he's an art teacher, she thinks she's a witch—hey, it's a mixed-up, screwed-up, crazy world, ain't it?

She continued sipping her soda in silence while Tommy was still letting out the odd chuckle.

"When I mentioned these cookies are good," she began, "that was a hint that I'd like another one."

Tommy grabbed a couple and passed the plate to her across the table, saying, "Only if you promise not to read my palm." He laughed at his own lame joke.

She just took the cookies and smiled, then said, "I don't need to read your palm."

"Go on then, fortune teller, what does my future hold?"

"You're obsessed with the future. You're always thinking about passing tests, going to college, getting a job as a reporter. In a way, you're already living in the future. You can probably guess your own future without help from me," said Sally Anne.

"So, I shouldn't think so much about the future. Is that what you're saying?"

"I didn't say that. But George would say that, wouldn't he?" said Sally Anne.

"Oh yes, your buddy George, whom you've known for all of one week," said Tommy rolling his eyes.

"But I'm right. He always says live for now—am I right?" she asked earnestly.

"Okay, so you're right. So what? So I'm focused on the future, George is focused on the present, and you're focused on...what...which one are you focused on?"

"Which one have you left out?" asked Sally Anne mischievously.

"Dunno, you tell me oh, soothsayer." Tommy was barely interested.

"The past," she said.

"What do you mean?" asked Tommy.

"The future is important," she said. "But George is right, too. You also have to live for the present."

"You sound more like an advice columnist than a witch."

"But the past," she continued, ignoring Tommy's mocking, "is important too."

"You mean childhood and all that? What are you, some kind of high school psychiatrist?"

"I'm a witch, remember? I'm not talking about earlier in this life," said Sally Anne. "I'm talking about past lives."

At this, Tommy just burst out laughing and he couldn't stop.

"I'm sorry, I'm sorry," he repeated between giggles and full-blown belly laughs.

Once Tommy's laughter had died down, Sally Anne reminded him about her painting in Mr. Bush's art class.

"I'm a good painter, aren't I?" she teased.

"But that doesn't make you a witch."

"I must be the quickest artist in the class, maybe even the world."

Tommy paused, the laughter was replaced now by silence. Eventually he said, "Okay, I admit that seemed spooky."

"And George's story about kissing me, didn't that make both of you think?" she said.

"How did you know about that?"

"I was in art class yesterday and wondered where both of you were. Then I sensed you were talking about me. True, I want you to know the truth about me—but no one else. So that's why I interrupted your little chat. Mr. Bush didn't even notice you weren't in class. I made that up to get you back to class and to stop talking about me. I was worried George might figure out the truth."

"The truth?" asked Tommy. "I don't think there was much danger of either of us figuring out that you were a witch."

"Maybe not," said Sally Anne. "But he did say that kissing me was like kissing a ghost, didn't he?"

"You weren't there when he said that. How do you know that?"

Tommy looked alarmed. First she had said she sensed he and George had been under the stairs. She could have stumbled upon them by chance. She'd said she sensed them talking about her. She'd kissed George the day before, so that was an educated guess on her part. But now she'd reminded Tommy that George had said kissing her was like kissing a ghost. That was pretty precise.

Sally Anne sat quietly. She emptied the last drops of her soda and set the glass on the counter.

"So which are you—a witch or a ghost?" asked Tommy challengingly.

"We're all ghosts, Tommy. We've all lived before. We're back here again to fix things that we got wrong last time."

"Isn't that what Buddhists believe?"

"It isn't just a Buddhist belief. But it doesn't really matter what people believe," said Sally Anne.

Tommy's mother was walking up the path to the back door. He could see her through the big window in the kitchen struggling with various grocery bags.

"What do you believe, Tommy?"

"I believe in the future, not the past," said Tommy, getting up to go and help his mother with the groceries. He looked back at Sally Anne as she was putting her coat on. He smiled at her.

She said, "One day, Tommy, you'll see that what you call your present life is just an illusion. Who's to say what is real?" Tommy was walking out the back door as she said this. He was anxious to introduce Sally Anne to his mother, providing she kept her witchy talk to herself.

"Hi, Mom," he said, taking some of the bags from her. "Here, let me help. By the way, I'd like to introduce you to a new classmate of mine. She likes your taste in cookies."

Tommy was talking excitedly. Although Sally Anne wasn't his girlfriend, he felt sure she would be one day.

"She?" asked Mrs. McDonald teasingly.

"Come on, Mom, she's just a friend," he whispered as they walked into the kitchen.

But the kitchen table was empty. "Well," said his mother.

"She was sitting right here," said Tommy. "Maybe she got nervous about meeting you and left," said Tommy, very annoyed at Sally Anne's rudeness, even if it was just nerves.

"Don't worry about it, son," she said. She started clearing away the table and said, "I thought you liked that new soda I bought."

"I do," replied Tommy.

"Well, why didn't you have a glass then?" his mother asked.

"I did," said Tommy, puzzled.

"Well, why is there just one glass on the table? Did you and your girlfriend—sorry, classmate—share the same glass?" inquired Mrs. McDonald.

"No, of course not."

"Well, if you had a glass and she had a glass, why is there only one glass?" Mrs. McDonald paused, looked at Tommy and said, "You don't need to make up stories, Tommy. You'll get around to bringing girls home soon enough. You don't need to try to impress the world by telling tales. There wasn't a girl here, was there, son?"

Tommy was flabbergasted.

"What? Why do you think I'd make up something like that? If I was going to make up a story, I'd tell you that I'd robbed a bank or had been to the moon. But having a soda and some cookies with a classmate...you've got to believe me, she was right there."

Then he remembered that she'd eaten a bunch of the cookies. "Here, look at this," he said, opening the

cookie jar. "Would I ever eat this many cookies?"

To his amazement, the jar was full.

"What is it, Tommy?" asked his mother.

"Nothing," said Tommy, staring at the full jar. "I think maybe I fell asleep and had a dream."

But of course he knew it was not a dream.

CHAPTER SIX

Yes!

Sally Anne sat beside Tommy the next morning in class.

"Okay," said Tommy. "I'm not sure if you're a witch, a ghost, or just a practical joker."

"What do you mean?" asked Sally Anne, feigning innocence.

"You win, I'm interested to hear more of your story and why you're here."

"What are you talking about, Tommy?" she asked impatiently.

"Yesterday? The case of the disappearing soda, the witch talk, your vanishing act? What do you think I'm talking about?" asked Tommy.

"Yesterday?"

"Yes, yesterday!"

"But you don't believe in the past, do you, Tommy? Maybe I was never in your house yesterday."

"Okay, I know something strange is going on. You've made your point, now can you tell me what your game is?"

"Okay, Tommy," said Sally Anne. "After school, why don't you come to my house and I'll explain everything."

"Should I be scared?" asked Tommy, smirking slightly.

"Yes!"

Tommy stopped smirking.

CHAPTER SEVEN

A Closer Look

At lunchtime, George saw Tommy walking around as if his head was in the clouds.

"Hey," he shouted at Tommy. "Stop pretending something interesting is going on inside that empty head of yours."

"Hi, George."

"Tommy, I was thinking about what you said about Sally Anne's painting. It is spooky, isn't it?" said George.

By now Tommy wanted to be the only one to know Sally Anne's secret. So he pretended that he'd solved the mystery of the fastest painter in school history.

"Well, I spoke to Sally Anne last night."

"Last night? You mean you talked to her outside of school?" asked George surprised.

"What's the big deal? She said she had done that same painting lots of times and that's what made it so easy for her to do it so quickly," lied Tommy.

"So, no mystery then?" asked George, sounding a little unconvinced.

"Nope."

"Well, maybe you're right, Tommy." George looked as if he was thinking.

"Now it's you who's pretending to have something interesting going on inside your head," commented Tommy.

"Did you look closely at that picture, Tommy?" asked George mysteriously.

"Not all that closely, why?" asked Tommy puzzled.

"Because you're in it!" said George.

George took Tommy to the art classroom

immediately. Mr. Bush was doing some paperwork at his desk. George knocked on the door.

"Come in," said Mr. Bush, adding, "if you must."

"Hello, sir, do you mind if we look at some of the paintings you've put on the wall this week?" asked George.

Mr. Bush regularly put recent paintings by students up on his wall. Not because he was interested, or appreciated his talented students, but to show Mrs. Lewis, the head of the art department, that his students actually did something. No doubt, he believed that this was because he was a wonderful teacher. Mrs. Lewis was once heard telling him that it was in spite of his teaching skills that his students achieved anything. Because he wasn't interested in his students' work, he hadn't looked at Sally Anne's picture very closely when he put it on the wall the day before.

"So, you've become an art critic?" said Mr. Bush suspiciously.

"No, not at all. Just looking for ways to improve my own work," said George.

"And you need Mr. McDonald to help you?" asked Mr. Bush.

"No," said Tommy, "I want to improve my work, too."

Mr. Bush looked piercingly at both of the boys. He remembered Mrs. Lewis saying that she was disappointed that he didn't encourage his students to take an interest in art. With this in mind, he said, "Okay, but don't make any noise, and don't be long."

Tommy looked at the painting. It was of an old village. There was a factory in the background and a boy and a girl on a cart being driven by a very old horse. The cart seemed to be carrying coal. It was a bleak painting, cloudy sky, dark colors, and sad people.

"Look at the boy on the cart," said George. He looked exactly like Tommy. But Tommy was looking at the girl on the cart who happened to look exactly

like Sally Anne. The boy and the girl were the only people smiling in the picture.

"That place looks so familiar," said Tommy.

"She must have a crush on you, Tommy," said George.

"Shhhhh!" said Mr. Bush.

"Come on, George," said Tommy, "let's go get something to eat."

CHAPTER EIGHT

===

Distracted

"Aren't you going to eat your fries?" asked George.

That was the first word between George and Tommy since they had looked at the picture. Tommy sat, deep in thought, at their table in the cafeteria.

"That picture seemed so familiar," said Tommy at last.

"Of course it was, you saw it in the art class the other day," said George.

"No, I don't mean the picture," said Tommy. "I mean the whole scene. I feel like I've been there before. The factory, the village—it all looked so familiar."

"Maybe you've seen it in a book or something..."

"That's it—in the dream!"

"What dream?" asked George.

"The dream I had the night before Sally Anne walked into our class."

"Oh, that dream," said George.

"Of course," replied Tommy. "It's too weird. I still can't make sense of it. I can't remember the dream very well, but the minute I saw Sally Anne, I was sure I recognized her. And now that picture. Maybe we have lived before."

"Lived before? What do you mean?"

"Nothing. I'll just ask her tonight."

"Tonight?" George was now exasperated. "What do you mean, tonight? Forget that, what do you mean 'lived before'? Maybe there is something interesting going on in that head of yours after all!"

"I'll tell you about it tomorrow—if it turns out it makes any sense," said Tommy.

Tommy was quiet for the rest of the day. He

barely heard George say goodbye as he took off for the bus. Tommy was too intrigued by Sally Anne, the picture, maybe living before, witches, and ghosts.

In the meantime, what Tommy did not know was that George was on the bus feeling very distracted. Why? Because when he kissed Sally Anne the other day, in addition to feeling like he was kissing a ghost, he felt like he was being transported back in time. In fact, he seemed to fall into a hypnotic trance and he vividly remembered the village, the factory, the old horse, and the girl on the cart. In other words, when George kissed Sally Anne, he seemed to be transported back in time, into the scene that Sally Anne painted in class. George had thought it had been his imagination, but, after having seen the painting again, he was now totally spooked. But when he was in his trance, he did not see anyone sitting beside the Sally Anne look-alike on the cart in the picture. George remembered her looking sad and alone. Besides that, the picture was pretty much a replica of the scene he remembered from his trance.

Of course, George—happy-go-lucky George—would not be the kind of boy to talk about trances. But he felt something was going on. Even Tommy—sensible Tommy McDonald—thought the picture was familiar. But, wondered George, where exactly did Tommy recognize the picture from? Just from his dream? There seemed to be more to it than that. George decided to act as if he wasn't all that interested in the whole thing. Nevertheless, he was secretly fascinated by it and could hardly wait to hear what Tommy had to say tomorrow.

CHAPTER NINE

The Kiss

Sally Anne crept up behind Tommy as he waited for her after school and shouted, "Gotcha!"

"For goodness' sake," screeched Tommy. Then he realized that it was only Sally Anne joking around.

"You're still not funny," he said sourly.

"Cheer up, you big wimp. Come on, we'll miss the train," she said, walking ahead of him.

"Train?" shouted Tommy after her.

"Yeah. I don't live in this part of town. Come on," she called back to Tommy.

If she didn't live in this part of town, thought Tommy, why did she go to this school?

They just barely made it to the train on time.

Sally Anne flashed her train pass to the conductor, who looked too bored to check it properly.

"You said earlier that I should be scared," said Tommy, not totally convinced that he should be.

"Well," she said, "that depends on how open-minded you are."

"What do you mean?" asked Tommy.

"I don't know if you're ready for this or not, but here goes nothing. Watch this."

Sally Anne stood up in the train compartment and walked to the door.

"Excuse me, everybody. Listen up," she shouted. "Everybody, listen to me, please."

Tommy was so embarrassed he sunk down in his seat as far as he could. Sally Anne continued.

"I'd like to sing you all a song." And she burst into "She loves you, yeah, yeah, yeah," lyrics from an old Beatles song. She even began dancing! Then she stood on a spare seat next to a very respectable, boring middle-aged man. She was clapping her hands and singing at the top of her lungs.

Tommy was mortified. He now closed his eyes and pretended to be asleep. Sally Anne saw and decided to draw attention to him.

"Listen up, folks. I've got some news for you. See that guy over there." Tommy knew she was pointing to his seat. "That's Tommy McDonald. He's never kissed a girl. Never!"

Shut up, shut up, shut up, said Tommy to himself, wondering what on earth had gotten into Sally Anne.

He nervously looked up, expecting to see the whole compartment full of people staring at him. To his amazement, everything was as before. No one had moved. In fact, they were all still doing what they had been doing before Sally Anne started her show. In fact, it looked like Sally Anne was invisible to them! He stood up and said, "Sally Anne..." but before he could continue, just about everyone in the compartment looked around to see why he was standing up and calling out a girl's name!

"They can't see or hear me," shouted Sally Anne.

"But they can hear me?" asked Tommy without thinking. And, of course, the other passengers looked at him once more, wondering if he was crazy.

"Yes, they can hear you all right. But not me. Watch this," said Sally Anne mischievously. She went right up to an old man without hair and said, "Hello baldy, where's your hair?"

Again, Tommy didn't think before he spoke and blurted out, "Sally Anne! Really! It's not his fault he doesn't have hair!"

The old man with no hair looked up at Tommy. "Are you talking about me, kid?"

"No, no, of course not," said Tommy.

Another bald man further down the carriage stood up and said angrily, "Well, in that case, the young rascal must be talking about me."

"No, no, honestly, it was a mistake. I'm sorry." Tommy was really confused now.

"Well then," said another man, taking his hat off, revealing his own bald head, "he must be talking about me."

It was like a nightmare. All three of the bald men got up from their seats and started walking slowly toward Tommy.

"You need a lesson in manners, young man," said one of them.

"Honestly, no, it was a mistake. I wasn't talking about any of you," he pleaded, stepping away from the advancing men.

"In that case," said the voice of a fourth man who had hair, "you must be talking about me!" And he put his hands up to his head and pulled at his hair. It was a wig! He too was bald!

"How did you know it was a wig? Who sent you? Are you spying on me?" asked the fourth man.

This is going from bad to worse, thought Tommy.

"How would I know you were bald? What do you mean spying? Sally Anne?" he cried out.

Suddenly, the train stopped. It was nowhere near a station. Suddenly, all the passengers were seated again. The man with the wig had his wig back on. The bald man with the hat had his hat back on. Both were reading newspapers as if nothing had happened. Tommy sat down quickly and wondered if it was all a dream.

The train started moving again. Sally Anne appeared beside Tommy. All that could be heard now was the noise of the train shuddering along the line.

"Did that really happen?" said Tommy to Sally Anne.

"Yes," said Sally Anne.

"But..." Tommy looked at everyone sitting as if nothing had happened. "Why are they..."

"They don't remember," interrupted Sally Anne.

"They don't remember?" said Tommy incredulously.

"They don't remember," repeated Sally Anne.

"How come?" asked Tommy.

"I handled it. Are you any closer to believing me—that I'm a witch?"

"I'm closer to going insane," said Tommy, completely at a loss. "How do I know," added Tommy, "that you didn't hypnotize me and none of that happened?"

"Fair question. You'll just have to trust me."

The train pulled into the station on a side of town that Tommy didn't recognize.

"Where are we?" asked Tommy, trying to come out of the daze brought on by the spooky incident on the train.

"We're in my hometown," said Sally Anne.

"I've never been here before," said Tommy.

She looked at him closely and smiled. "Are you sure nothing seems familiar?" she asked.

Tommy looked around and looked for something to recognize. He vaguely recognized the general outlay of the main street, but then again all small towns tended to look a little alike. "No, I don't think so," he said.

"Well, you should. This is where you were born," said Sally Anne.

"But I was born in Belldale. That's miles from here," he said.

"Maybe in this life, but in your previous life, you were born here."

"Sorry, I don't believe in all this stuff—too far-fetched."

"Oh, really, well I can think of a lot of far-fetched things that you believe."

"Like what?"

"You believe in the future. You believe you're going to be a journalist, go to college, and lots of other things," she said.

"So, I know where I'm going. So do lots of people," said Tommy. "What's wrong with that?"

"I didn't say there's anything wrong with it, but if you believe in the future why not the past? Do you need more proof?"

Tommy thought about her disappearing act at his house and the train journey. But even though these things spooked him, he wasn't certain that Sally Anne was a witch. She might just be a mixed-up girl with nothing better to do. But why bring him into it? Why me? he thought.

"Okay then, if you're offering more proof, then fire away," he challenged, although he was a little apprehensive.

Sally Anne looked disappointed, and then after thinking for a few moments, she said, "Okay, watch this."

Sally Anne reached out her hands to Tommy's face and held it for a moment, then kissed him.

Tommy didn't have time to react and, before he knew it, his mind was whirling. Sally Anne stepped back and Tommy opened his eyes but he was stunned to find himself in a very different setting. He couldn't believe his eyes. He was in the exact

same place. There were signs on store windows saying Rolwell Bakery and so on, but everybody in the street was dressed in old-fashioned clothes—very old-fashioned clothes. Victorian, in fact. He was then hit by very strange smells. Then he realized that there were no cars, only horse-drawn carriages. Then he noticed that the road wasn't paved, it was just dust, like in an old Wild West movie. The noises he heard were from horses, carts moving, drivers cracking their whips. It was like he had been thrown back in time! Then he looked at Sally Anne and saw her dressed in the same old-fashioned dress that he remembered from the painting she'd done in Mr. Bush's art class. He felt dizzy. His mind was trying to make sense of what was going on.

"Wake up," he said aloud to himself. "Wake up, Tommy!"

"You are awake, Tommy. More awake than you normally are. What you call waking hours isn't as awake as this. This is real Tommy," said Sally Anne.

He looked around and immediately recognized the old factory from the painting. In fact, everything was exactly the same as in the painting. Suddenly Tommy noticed his clothes felt different and he looked down and realized that he was dressed exactly as the boy in Sally Anne's painting. The same flat cap on his head, the same brown pants with braces, the same white striped collarless shirt. "This can't be real! It can't be! It can't be!"

Tommy felt like he was falling asleep. "It can't be, can't be, can't be...can't..."

CHAPTER TEN

The Cap

"Wake up, Tommy, wake up." Mrs. McDonald was shaking her son.

"It can't be," Tommy was still muttering to himself.

"Wake up, Tommy," said his mother again.

Tommy opened his eyes but found it hard to wake up. "Where am I?" he mumbled, utterly confused.

"You're in bed, where do you think you are? Hurry and get up! You'll be late. Come on, Tommy, this is not like you. What's going on with you these days?" asked Mrs. McDonald.

"I wish I knew," said Tommy.

"What?"

"Nothing," he replied drowsily.

Could it be, thought Tommy, that Sally Anne, the girl who sat beside him in school, really was a witch? How did he get to bed last night? How did he get home? Was it all a dream? After all, he'd dreamed about Sally Anne before.

As he was getting dressed, thinking about all the recent strangeness, he heard his mother shouting to his father.

"David, is this your cap?"

"Cap? I don't wear a cap. Do you think I'm my old man or something?"

"Or something," shouted Tommy downstairs.

"Very funny," shouted Dad. "Is this yours, Tommy?"

"Of course it isn't," he heard his mom say sharply to his dad.

Then it struck Tommy. Of course it was his cap! He remembered wearing it when he was mysteriously taken back in time. But how could he be sure?

"Yeah, it is mine actually," said Tommy, grabbing the cap from the breakfast table. He ran out the door, saying, "I'm going to be late." Then he disappeared out into the street.

Obviously, thought Tommy, my parents haven't asked any questions about yesterday. I must have come home on time. Otherwise, they'd be asking questions.

Sally Anne was absent that day.

Darn, thought Tommy, I wanted to ask her some questions. He waited until he was in art class later that day before he looked at Sally Anne's painting. He wanted to check the cap on the boy in the cart to see if it was the same one in his house that morning. That way he'd know for certain if there really was some connection between the picture and his experiences the previous day. Where was Sally Anne?

He really wanted to ask her what the heck was going on. And what the heck does she want with me, he thought, yet again.

He was the first person in art class. He'd dodged George as the class made their way from math to art. He wanted to look at the picture on his own. Tommy glanced around to make sure no one was paying any attention to him and then opened his backpack. He took out the cap and held it up beside the painting. But the painting was different!

Tommy couldn't believe his eyes. I must be looking at the wrong picture, he thought. But no, it was signed by Sally Anne. She must have snuck in and replaced the original. Somehow, he knew deep down that wasn't true. The new picture showed the same boy and girl, but they were both on a chariot! In fact, the people walking beside the chariot looked like Vikings. There were no real buildings, only what looked like straw huts.

Tommy wondered whether he should go see

the school nurse and confess that he had lost it! She must have changed the picture. It was the only explanation. It couldn't have changed itself—could it? Tommy didn't know what to believe anymore.

He sat down, more confused than before. George sat down beside him.

"Did I do something wrong?" asked George.

"No, why?"

"Because I don't think you've said two words to me all day. What's the matter? Too busy thinking about your future again?" teased George.

"Worrying about my past, actually," replied Tommy.

"What are you talking about now?" laughed George.

"George, go and look at Sally Anne's picture after class."

"Why?"

"Just look."

"Okay, okay."

CHAPTER ELEVEN

You're Not the One

At the end of class, most of the students filed out quickly. Mr. Bush saw George and Tommy looking at Sally Anne's picture.

"What is it that fascinates you about that picture?" he asked gruffly.

"Did Sally Anne paint this picture recently?" asked George.

"Are you kidding? You were here when she did it, weren't you?"

"But that's not the same one," said Tommy, pointing to the new one on the wall.

"Of course it is," said Mr. Bush.

"You mean no one's switched them out?"

Tommy was interrupted by Mr. Bush. "Get out of here. Go on, go to your next class, you two. Of course no one's switched them out. What kind of prank would that be? Shouldn't you be popping your pimples or worrying about BO or spraying on body spray or whatever it is you kids are doing these days?" shouted Mr. Bush as he ushered them out of his classroom. "Don't hurry back. Next time bring your senses, please."

And with that, Mr. Bush slammed the door.

"Cranky old man," said George.

"Perhaps we could get Sally Anne to put a spell on him," said Tommy, laughing for the first time that day.

"Yeah, like she's a witch," laughed George, not knowing how true it might be. "Prettiest witch I've ever seen," he added.

"Really, and yet for some reason you stopped chasing her after your first kiss," said Tommy slyly.

George got quiet.

Tommy realized that he might get some clues from George by asking him for the full story of what happened between George and Sally Anne. So he asked George for the facts. George simply told him that he and Sally Anne had a short kiss and that was that. George again mentioned that something spooky happened but he had trouble remembering it all.

"In fact," George said, "I can't remember what really happened and what was a dream. I'm not sure if I didn't imagine the whole thing. The only thing I remember was her last words that night."

"What were they?" asked Tommy eagerly.

"She just said, 'No, you're not the one after all.'"

"At least she's honest," said Tommy cruelly.

"No, I mean it was like she was looking for someone in particular."

"Aren't we all, man!"

"No, but it was as if she could only tell from the kiss."

"You're not making any sense, George," pretended Tommy. But, of course, George was making perfect sense to Tommy.

But really, there was only one person who could make sense of the whole picture. Where, thought Tommy, was Sally Anne?

CHAPTER TWELVE

4,1,8,1

"How was school today?" asked Tommy's mom when she came in.

"Fine," said Tommy automatically.

"I meant to ask you this morning, Tommy, where did you get that cap?" asked Tommy's mom.

"From the olden days," said Tommy, getting up from the kitchen table to go to his room.

"Very funny," said his mom, a little curious.

Tommy was lying on his bed, scanning his bookshelves. He was trying to distract himself from the growing mystery of the witch, Sally Anne, if she really was a witch.

Just then, he saw a picture of Sally Anne in his

mind and closed his eyes to see it more clearly.
She was picking up a phone. Am I dreaming? he
wondered, trying to snap out of it. Am I imagining
this? His head felt strained. He had a vision of Sally
Anne dialing numbers on a phone. He tried to see
what the numbers were, but he could only make out
the last four digits: 4, 1, 8, 1.

Hey, he thought, that's the last four digits of my
telephone number!

Just then, the vision disappeared and Tommy
could hear the phone ringing downstairs.

He heard his father pick it up.

"Hello," said his dad. "Yes, one second...Tommy!"
he shouted. "It's for you."

Tommy was numb. Wow! Perhaps there is
something to this whole witch thing after all. He
was trying to make light of it. Anyway, it couldn't be
Sally Anne. She didn't even know his number.

It has to be George, he thought.

As he was walking down the stairs, he heard his

mom ask his dad who was on the phone for Tommy.

Tommy's dad replied, "She says it's an old girlfriend."

"An old one!" exclaimed his mother. "Tommy's never had a girlfriend, at least not as far as I know."

Tommy looked at the phone lying on the table. Should he pick it up? His mother was right. He'd never had a girlfriend. At least he thought, half joking, at least not in this life. He picked it up.

"Hello."

"Hello, Tommy." It was Sally Anne!

"That's right, Tommy, not in this life," she said, as if she had just read Tommy's mind.

"We have to talk," he said impatiently.

"Who's that girl on the phone, Tommy?" shouted his mother, getting up from her chair.

"You have a girl stashed away that you haven't told us about!" shouted his dad, also getting up.

"We'll have to get that phone tapped," laughed Mrs. McDonald. "It's the only way we'll find out what's going on around here," she added.

"Tommy," called Sally Anne into the phone, trying to get Tommy's attention. "Meet me at the train station in an hour."

"How did you get my number?"

But she'd already hung up.

The train station!

Reasons to be worried, thought Tommy, one: she knows my number. Two: it's dark. Three: that last train ride with Sally Anne drove me crazy. Four: it's raining and I'll get wet. Five: Mom and Dad are way too interested in what they think is my love life. Six: I don't have a love life. Seven: I'm panicking. While counting up the reasons to be worried, he had gone up the stairs, changed into his jeans and at the same time, fended off question after question from his nosy parents.

"Tommy, you're not listening. Where are you going?" said his mom.

"Is something wrong, son?" asked his dad as

Tommy jumped down the last few stairs on the stairway.

"I think there is something wrong, Jean," he heard his dad's now distant voice say to his mother.

What a detective, thought Tommy sarcastically. Eight: my parents are dumb! Nine: where does that leave me?! Ten: what the heck am I doing out here?

He was now at the station. He was about half an hour early. He was soaking wet. He was tired and confused. The half hour passed slowly, but it passed. Eleven: here comes Sally Anne!

CHAPTER THIRTEEN

Should I Be Scared?

"Okay," said Tommy full of purpose. "What's going on? This mystery has to be solved tonight."

"It will be," said Sally Anne.

"Okay, start talking," said Tommy.

"You're so difficult to convince, Tommy. You won't believe me if I just tell you. I want to show you once more what you are calling strange things. I think it's the only way I can persuade you of my reason for being here."

"I don't know if I can take anymore. The last two days seem like a blur. I feel like I haven't slept at all. I have so much to explain to my parents and George. But what can I explain? I don't have a clue," said

Tommy, running his hands through his hair.

"Tommy, if only you had faith. Then I wouldn't have had to put you through all this."

"I feel so disorientated," said Tommy. Then he shook his head.

"No, that's not the right word," said Sally Anne. "All that's really happened to you is that you've had your mind opened..."

"You can say that again!" said Tommy.

"...for the better. How can you understand life's mysteries if you don't have an open mind?"

"Well then," said Tommy, his voice sounding bitter, "is my mind open enough yet?"

"Almost."

Tommy sighed and then said, "What if I just say goodbye and not give all this stuff a second thought? What if I told you to leave me alone? All this would be forgotten, wouldn't it? And if that's the case, then it's not important, is it? I don't have to go through this. I don't care if you're a witch anymore. I just want to go back to my normal life. The one I was certain about before you came around."

"You can run, but you can't hide. I've chased you through the centuries, not because I want to— because I have to!"

"Chased me through the centuries!" exclaimed Tommy. "This just gets worse." He paused. "I'm trying to believe you. I want to figure this out! I want to understand! But I can't. I just can't accept all this stuff."

"That's why we are going on one last train ride to Rolwell. I knew you wouldn't believe me. This time, if you really want to solve this puzzle, you'll have to do what I say."

"And if I don't..."

"And if you don't, I'll leave you alone for the rest of this life. And you'll be a journalist. A successful one. You'll have everything you want, within reason. But in your old age, you'll wonder about this moment. It will prey on your mind. It will become more important to you as you realize that you only have a few years left. You will feel frustration that you didn't check it out. That frustration will sour your last years. You'll realize, as most people do when they are running out of time, that one of the purposes of your life was to face all questions, with or without fear. All your journalistic triumphs will appear meaningless beside your regrets. Because, no matter what you achieve, you'll believe you could have achieved more. And if only you'd faced this moment with courage, perhaps you'd have discovered a great secret. When you wonder what life was all about, you'll wish you had explored every mystery thoroughly."

Tommy was listening. He knew how to plan his future, but he knew what Sally Anne was saying was true. He could visualize himself an old man, sitting in a comfortable chair, on a freshly cut lawn, in some beautiful sun-drenched garden, pondering his life. He knew it would bother him that he never followed up on what almost any journalist would consider a great story.

He also knew that somehow he'd have missed a chance to explore the potential of past lives, clairvoyance, ghosts, and everything that the world had wanted for centuries to know more about.

Sally Anne stood staring at him, waiting for Tommy to agree to come on the train. The rain was still pouring down on them. They were on the platform and the noise of the train coming into the station interrupted Tommy's thoughts. He knew now that he had to face whatever mystery was behind all this.

"Should I be scared?" he asked again, knowing the answer. But he was resigned to boarding the train anyway.

"That depends on how open your mind is," said Sally Anne, faintly smiling.

Tommy reached out and opened the train door for Sally Anne. She boarded and looked around for

Tommy. He was still on the platform. He seemed to be gathering up all his courage before he followed her. The train started moving. He jumped on.

They found seats and sat down.

"Why Rolwell?" asked Tommy. "What's the significance of Rolwell?"

"Like I said," replied Sally Anne, "it's your hometown. I can show you around, and I know it will gradually become more familiar to you the more we talk.

"Do you mean I really have lived before?"

"Yes. Lots of times."

"You too?" he asked.

"Of course. Everybody on this train has. Everybody in the world has."

"What for?" asked Tommy.

"Easy, Tommy. I may be a witch, a winter witch to be specific, but that doesn't mean I can solve the riddle of what life is all about," she laughed.

"But you know more about it than me," said

Tommy, who was hoping for more enlightenment than Sally Anne was so far offering.

"Well, I can make you aware of the rights and wrongs of our past lives. I can point out what changes you wanted to make in your last life. I don't know it all, but I know that we live again in order to have another chance to succeed at the things we failed at last time. We all have to move on, but if we're stuck at the same place, every lifetime, we need help to overcome whatever it is that's holding us back."

"This is heavy. I can't pretend to understand all you're telling me," said Tommy.

Sally Anne thought for a moment then said, "Watch this. See that guy sitting there beside the window?" she asked, pointing across to the other side of the carriage.

"Yeah…" replied Tommy suspiciously.

"I can show you a short history of him. I can show you what he looked like in his past lives."

Tommy was not about to challenge her after all he'd been through and he was curious to see this.

"Okay," he said. "Let's see. If nothing else, this will be a unique way to pass the time!" Tommy was trying to sound skeptical, but Sally Anne knew he wasn't really skeptical anymore. Still, it couldn't do any harm.

"First," she said, "you have to kiss me."

"What?!"

"Tommy, you and I are linked by a love that is very, very old. The power of it has built up over many centuries. This power is unique and special. It is this force that enables me to show you all these strange things. That is why you have to kiss me."

Tommy thought about it. He was his typical analytical self. He thought Sally Anne's statement sounded logical. He also noticed that he wasn't really scared anymore. Just curious, very curious. So, for that reason, he leaned in close to her and put his hand on her back and said, "Come here, then."

Sally Anne moved forward, and they kissed. Instantly, Tommy fell back into his seat. He could see stars. The colors of everything around him were changing by the second. The man that Sally Anne had pointed to earlier seemed to glow. Slightly at first, then gradually, his dull, drab brown overcoat seemed to be a bright yellow light surrounding him. The man continued to stare out the train window, unaware of anything strange occurring. All the colors of him—his pink skin, his black hair, his green eyes, his red nose—all seemed to become incredibly bright, and brighter, and brighter, until there was an immense explosion of color and sparks flying all around him, as if he'd exploded. But the man was still unaware of anything happening.

Tommy heard Sally Anne's voice saying, "That explosion is how we—how can I explain? —tune into him. The ride gets a little rougher here, Tommy, so hold on to your seat a little tighter now." Then he heard her laugh as if this was all a game!

Tommy looked again at the man. He seemed to be younger. He had originally looked as if he was about thirty-five, but now he was about twenty-five. He had a different suit on, a brighter one.

But now he seemed to be getting even younger again, right in front of Tommy's eyes.

Tommy blinked and the man was now a boy about his own age. Tommy was trying not to blink now in case he missed anything.

Now he was a toddler.

Now he was a baby.

Tommy couldn't keep up with the pace. He heard a slight boom and the baby seemed to explode in bright colors.

Now there was just dust. It cleared to reveal a man in a soldier's uniform from World War II!

But still he was getting younger but at a much quicker pace than before. It was almost like watching a blur, constantly changing.

Another boom and the soldier was now a soldier

from what looked like George Washington's time.

Boom. Now he was a child dressed in rags from Shakespeare's time. All the while the man was changing, his skin was stretching and shrinking, his face was growing larger, getting smaller, all at such a fast pace.

Sally Anne's voice then said, "Look around the carriage."

All the people in the carriage were undergoing the same transformations. All their past lives were flashing before Tommy's eyes!

All of a sudden, the train stopped with a jolt. Now, instead of the people on the train just sitting down, they all seemed to get up and start acting out all their past lives' important experiences!

The men who had been soldiers in past lives were covered in blood. Tommy could see them getting hit by bullets. He saw them contort their faces in pain. He heard them scream.

He saw other men fighting with swords, as if they

were from the days of pirates. He saw the swords entering flesh as the pirates fought each other to the death. All these horrific scenes were going on all at once. All changing instantly into other scenes as the past lives of the other passengers on the train unfolded before Tommy's eyes.

The scenes were so real. He could smell the sea, the fields, the blood, everything. It was becoming too much for him. He had his eyes closed but remarkably it made no difference. He could still see it all. He put his hands over his ears, but he could still hear it all. He screamed, but nothing changed. Even with his eyes shut, he could see that the other passengers, all in some terrible scenes from past lives, heard his scream.

The pirates grinned and started walking toward him. The soldiers pointed their rifles at him. They were all screaming at him, their voices filled with hate. Ugly faces, contorted in pain and in fear, were only feet away when he heard Sally Anne's voice say,

"Shout 'To the end of your life!' to them. Hurry, Tommy!"

Tommy, without hesitating, shouted, "To the end of your life!"

All the horrible scenes from the passengers' past lives exploded at that very instant. Pieces of them flew against the windows, chairs, and doors. Everything was splattered in blood and goo.

Just then, the train jolted forward. Tommy blinked. When his eyes reopened, it was as if nothing had happened. He was breathless and panting. One or two of the other passengers, now all looking completely normal, looked around at him. Then they carried on reading their papers, chatting or just looking out the window.

Sally Anne was looking at him, concerned.

Again, the only noise to be heard was the sound of the train moving along the line.

Tommy looked out the window. It was daylight. Bright, sunny daylight! But when he and Sally Anne had boarded the train, it was nine o'clock, dark, and raining.

"Are you all right?" he heard Sally Anne ask.

"Should I be after that?" asked Tommy.

"That depends."

"On what?"

"On how determined you are to figure out your past," she said.

"After that, very determined!" he said, at last utterly convinced that he was in the grip of forces more powerful than himself.

"Well, in that case, you'll be all right."

"I'm relieved to hear it!"

Tommy sat there thinking furiously. Maybe it was a trick. No. No way. It was too real. Every time a doubt crept into his mind, he just needed to look out the window at the broad daylight at—he checked his watch—9:45 p.m.

The train pulled into Rolwell station and all the passengers rose from their seats. If Tommy had any doubts before, they were all gone now.

He whispered tentatively to Sally Anne as they stepped onto the platform, "Were my past lives as eventful as the ones you just showed me?"

"Yes. Oh, yes. That's why we're here," she said ominously.

CHAPTER FOURTEEN

The Truth

"Come and meet my family," said Sally Anne as they walked away from the station.

"Why do I feel like I'm on the way to meet the Addams family?" Tommy said quietly.

They walked for some time until they came to the gate of a beautiful large old house. There were other similar houses nearby.

They walked up the path together and Sally Anne produced a key from her pocket to unlock the door.

"I live here with many relatives. I like big families, don't you?" she asked.

"Depends on the family," replied Tommy. "I know some families that I wish were much smaller!"

As they walked through the hallway of Sally Anne's home, Tommy wondered where everybody was.

"They are out at work," said Sally Anne, reading his mind again. She smiled and said, "Something to drink?"

She told Tommy to sit down at the breakfast bar in the kitchen. He did. Then he said, "No. Nothing for me. Let's get to the point."

"Well," she said looking at him kindly, "you're as ready as you'll ever be!"

She sat opposite him and said, "Are you sure you're not thirsty or hungry? This may take a while."

"No. The sooner we start, the sooner we'll finish," said Tommy matter-of-factly.

"Okay then. Here goes nothing. I am a winter witch. That means I have what people foolishly call supernatural powers. These powers are, in fact, very natural, and we were all born with them many, many thousands of years ago. But as we evolved as humans, the spiritual side of our nature regressed. In other words, the better we got physically, the worse we got spiritually."

"Hold on," said Tommy. "That's a lot of big words."

"How come? You know what a spirit is, don't you?"

"Yes."

"Okay. Then you understand. Anyway, my story—or should I say—our story started in Ancient Egypt."

"Slow down! What? This is a lot to take in," pleaded Tommy.

"You were a prince. I was a servant girl. You treated me kindly when everyone else treated me cruelly. I promised you when you died that I'd always help you even in your future lives."

"How did I die?" asked Tommy.

"Your father, the king, had you put to death because you wouldn't let them put me to death.

They said I was a sorcerer, which was true. But as I've said, I was a winter witch. That means I only use my powers to help people."

"I know what a winter witch is…"

"So, you tried to explain that I was helping people but they took great offense to that."

"Why?"

"Because I was a servant—low class. How dare I offer to help kings? And of course, they were scared of my powers. The king wasn't a totally bad man. He knew you'd live again. But these were bad times. You were traumatized by the fact your own father ordered your death. The night before they killed you, we talked all night. You were in a dungeon. But I visited you in spirit. You were terrified. I promised to always be with you."

Tommy sat in stunned stillness. Tears were sliding down his silent face. She wiped them. Then she kissed him.

He felt himself relax. He felt as if he was drifting

out of his body. In a moment, he was in the sky with the stars. He seemed to be flying. He felt the cold air, the swoosh of his own speed as he effortlessly drifted over continents that looked like tiny stains below him. He felt the pull of the earth as he was dragged down. In an instant, he was in a dark, clay dungeon. It was small and stuffy with just a stick with a flame at the end—an ancient torch—hanging somehow on the wall.

He smelled smells he hadn't smelled for thousands of years and yet he felt as if he'd never been away from this lonely dim cell. He felt fear rise within him. Then he had a vision of Sally Anne. She was telling him that everything would be all right, that there was an afterlife.

"No there isn't," he heard himself say.

"There is, you've got to believe me. We'll meet again. You've saved me. So I'll save you."

He felt doubt. But he seemed to be aware of more than this. It was as if he was trying to tell himself that he knew for sure there was an afterlife.

Gradually, fear left him. The torch on the wall burned lower. A door opened. Two rough men in Egyptian clothes took hold of him and dragged him out. He didn't struggle. He just smiled. He knew for sure that he would see the servant girl again. He knew she would save him. If not this time, then in some other world, some other time. Then he seemed to feel tremendous pain all over. But instantly, it was gone. Now he was in space again. Unafraid, dreaming, drifting, remembering that he was Tommy McDonald, soon to be award-winning journalist, but now one not afraid of the past!

He felt a kiss on his lips. He opened his eyes, as if they'd been sealed! Sally Anne pulled back and smiled across the breakfast bar at him.

"Sally Anne, I—I don't know what to say...This is incredible. Me? A prince?"

"Well, not now, Tommy," she said, trying to bring him back to earth. "You were, long ago. We've all had our great moments in history. But that's not the point. We've got to remember what scared us most. Fear stops us from developing. We have to confront our greatest fear..."

"You mean like spiders?" interrupted Tommy.

"What!"

"I'm scared of spiders, all bugs actually..."

"Excuse me, I'm trying to be serious here," said Sally Anne.

"Okay, okay. Let's see if I've got this right. You are a witch."

"A winter witch," she corrected him.

"A winter witch. This I believe. So why have you appeared to save me now?" he asked curiously. He was still confused as to why it had taken him thousands of years to be rescued.

"Because, you are stubborn!" she said. "When the Romans were in Britain, you were too busy studying to be a great road engineer! You wouldn't believe who I was. When the Armada was being prepared in

Spain to attack England, I was a Romani traveler in Spanish villages. You were a young volunteer soldier, lying about your age to join the Spanish army. The scene from the picture I painted in Mr. Bush's class—that was the last time I made contact with you. You were a coal seller..."

"A coal cellar?"

"No, I mean you sold coal from a cart."

"But how come I don't remember?"

"Because every time, in every lifetime, I met you and 'freaked you out' as you would say. We always got to the point of discovery and you would lose your nerve."

"Like tonight, before we got on the train?"

"That's right. You always were so practical. Always worried about the future. You didn't want to get involved in things that would interfere with your future. And yes, you were always successful, but your old age was always filled with regret."

"What was the difference this time then?" asked

Tommy confused.

"This time, I used more of my powers. This time I used magic, like on the train."

"Why didn't you use that before?" inquired Tommy.

"Because every time I use my powers, it lessens them a little."

"You mean that my lack of faith has weakened you!" said Tommy worried.

"Yes," was the blunt, honest answer.

Tommy paused long and hard before eventually saying, "Sorry. I'm really sorry."

"You can make up for it by acknowledging that there is more to life than this life," said Sally Anne.

"Does that mean this life is not important—like it doesn't matter if I graduate or do well?" said Tommy, suddenly enjoying the possibility that life could be a lot of fun without worry!

"Of course it matters. You have to try your best at whatever you do. Anything else is a waste of time—

precious time. But remember that there is more. Anyway, I've now told you the whole story. Do you believe me?" She looked very worried. She was frowning.

"Yes," said Tommy immediately. "Yes. Without a doubt. I recognize all the lives you've described."

"I hope so. Because you won't always remember," said Sally Anne.

"Why not? I'm not very likely to forget all this, am I?"

"Yes. And you'll wonder if it was all a dream."

"But you'll always be in school to remind me. Won't you?" he asked.

"Even if I'm not, I'll be around. Somewhere." She looked at her watch. "Come on," she said, "you'll miss the last train back."

"But there's so much to say! Can't we talk some more...?"

"You don't understand. The next train really is the last."

Tommy instinctively knew what she meant. It really would be the last train back.

"But we'll talk tomorrow, right?" he asked as they walked quickly toward the station.

"I might not be there tomorrow."

"Well, the next day? Some time?"

She looked at him as he purchased his ticket and said, "Some time. Yes. Some time."

"Great. I can't wait," said Tommy.

CHAPTER FIFTEEN

No More Secrets

As Tommy made his way home, he was delirious. What was he going to say to his parents? Where have you been? he imagined them asking. How could he reply that he had not only been to different places but completely different times! Oh, never mind, he said to himself, this will be my secret. Our secret he thought he heard Sally Anne's voice say.

"Okay," he replied out loud. "Our secret."

"Where have you been?" exclaimed his parents, one after the other, as he tried unsuccessfully to sneak in the front door.

"Out," he replied.

"Thank you. That really clears up that mystery for

us," said his angry mother. Just then, the phone rang.

"Hello!" said Mrs. McDonald annoyed that her inquisition had been interrupted. There was a pause as Mrs. McDonald listened.

"Oh...I see...okay then Mrs. Dickens...Yes...thank you for calling." She put down the phone.

"Who was that?" asked Mr. McDonald.

"That was Mrs. Dickens, Sally Anne's mother."

"Oh, the old girlfriend's mother," said Mr. McDonald, now smiling. "So that's where he's been. On a date?"

"Helping her with homework, according to Mrs. Dickens."

Tommy's mother looked suspiciously at him.

"Yeah," said Tommy, grasping the lifeline that Sally Anne's mother had thrown him. "That's right. She's the new girl. The homework is a little tough for her, so I'm helping her. I really was."

Mrs. McDonald looked relieved.

"We thought you'd joined a gang or something.

Up to no good. And by the way, I don't believe for a minute you were doing just homework. Is this girl pretty?"

"I haven't really noticed," said Tommy blushing.

His mom and dad burst into laughter.

As he was walking up the stairs, his mom shouted up, "No more secrets, young man. Do you hear me?"

"Yes," he replied, then saying to himself, "no more secrets."

CHAPTER SIXTEEN

Four Points

Sally Anne wasn't at school the next day. Miss Sharpe said it turned out that Sally Anne's dad got another job, better than the one he'd taken in this area.

Tommy was not surprised. He'd thought about it all night. She'd done her part. The rest was now up to him.

"Bummer about Sally Anne," said George at lunch.

"Yeah."

"Life goes on though, huh?"

"Yeah, that's for sure."

"So, did you kiss her?" asked George, determined

to discover the secret behind Tommy's obvious new confidence.

"Yeah, as a matter of fact, I did."

"Yes!" shouted George. "Tommy McDonald has finally scored a point!"

"Four times."

"Four points! You've finally grown up!" exclaimed George.

"Countless times," replied Tommy.

CHAPTER SEVENTEEN

The Ticket

Out of curiosity, Tommy went to the school library after his last class. He was looking for a map of the whole area. He found one. He had an idea that he wouldn't find what he was looking for. And he didn't. He was looking for Rolwell, Sally Anne's home. His hometown, she'd said. But he knew that was just a made up reason to get him to go there. Nowhere on the map did it mention Rolwell. It didn't exist, but he wasn't worried.

That night, he went to the train station. He looked at all the destinations. Rolwell wasn't on the board. Or in the schedule. No railway staff had heard of it. He wasn't surprised.

On the way out of the station, he saw a man at the taxi line. Tommy recognized the man. The man got into a taxi and caught Tommy's eye.

"Don't lose your train ticket," he called out to Tommy. "You might need to help someone one day."

The taxi disappeared around a corner.

"My ticket?" Tommy wondered. Then he searched in his jeans pocket. He pulled out a crumpled piece of paper. It was a ticket. He looked at the destination part of the ticket. It said Rolwell.

Many times, in the years to come, Tommy wondered whether he'd had a nervous breakdown or something around the time Sally Anne had come into his life. He remained friends with George for years, and they rarely spoke about Sally Anne. They never discussed the mysterious side of it all. Mr. Bush, at the end of that semester, threw out all the students' artwork, so Tommy never even got the chance to examine Sally Anne's painting again.

But whenever he'd convinced himself that he had imagined the whole thing, he went to the top drawer of his desk in his bedroom and pulled out the train ticket. That's what kept it all real in his mind.

He still dreamed about Sally Anne, and she told him in these dreams that she was happy. Because he believed the whole story, and he did, she was able to regain all her witch's strength and continue to help others who were lost in time.

Tommy still worked hard, but he lived for the present. He still worried sometimes about the future, but he never again worried about the past.

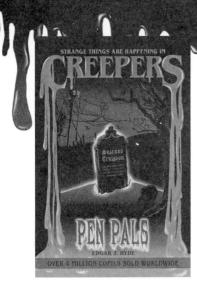
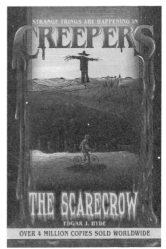
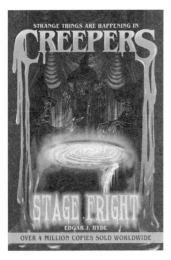

tles in the Creepers series!

The Piano
ISBN: 9781486718764

Cold Kisser
ISBN: 9781486718740

The Gravedigger
ISBN: 9781486718795

Edgar J. Hyde has a message just for you.
If you solve his riddles, prepare for some creepy fun,
and you might even find a surprise waiting for you…
Solve the riddles on the next page and in Pen Pals,
unscramble the letters, and fill in the blanks of this web URL

www.flowerpotpress.com/_ _ _ _ _ _ _

with the answers you find. Go to the website
with your parent's permission and find out
what waits on the other side.

Read
in
Peace

1. Have you been studying and paying attention
in class, or have you been off on a witchy adventure?
To find the answer to this riddle, simply go to
the page number of the answer to this math problem
and look at the first letter on the page.
14+(2 x 20)−(10−4)+(5 x 5)= Page ?

2. Some friendships have stood the test of time and
have lasted years. Some since the two were children.
But in some instances, friendships can go as far back as centuries.
For Tommy and Sally Anne, they were friends hundreds of years ago.
What letter does the country they first met in start with?

3. Tommy is a strange young man. He is always caught up
in thoughts of kissing and a future that is yet to exist.
But one thing that is true about Tommy is his name.
What letter does Tommy's last name start with?

CREEPERS

"The language, vocabulary, sentence complexity, text structure, plot and character development, use of scattered illustrations, length, and generous font and spacing are inviting and non-threatening.

The content and ideas are
DARK, THRILLING, SPINE-CHILLING, GRUESOME
at times, extremely interesting, and sometimes even hilarious.

Middle school and high school readers looking for high-interest stories involving revolting witches, mystery, drama, crushes, cliques and other tween/teen coming of age themes will devour these books.
And leave you thinking...
This could never happen, **OR COULD IT?**"

—Marla Conn, M.S. Ed., reading and literacy specialist and educational consultant